Mog and Barnaby

Mog and Barnaby

Judith Kerr

HarperCollins *Children's Books*

"Who's this?"

"Wake up,
Mog!"

"Look what's in here.

It's Barnaby!"

"He wants…

"He won't hurt you!

He likes you!"

"He wants to be...

"He'd like to
stay with you
always…

He has to go
home for his
lunch now."

"Dear Mog!"

"Dear Mog!"

First published in hardback in Great Britain by William Collins Sons & Co Ltd in 1991
First published in paperback by Picture Lions in 1992
This paperback edition first published by HarperCollins Children's Books in 2016
Picture Lions and HarperCollins Children's Books are divisions of HarperCollins Publishers Ltd

1 3 5 7 9 10 8 6 4 2
ISBN: 978-0-00-817116-2

Visit our website at www.harpercollins.co.uk

Printed and bound in China

A selection of bestselling picture books by Judith Kerr

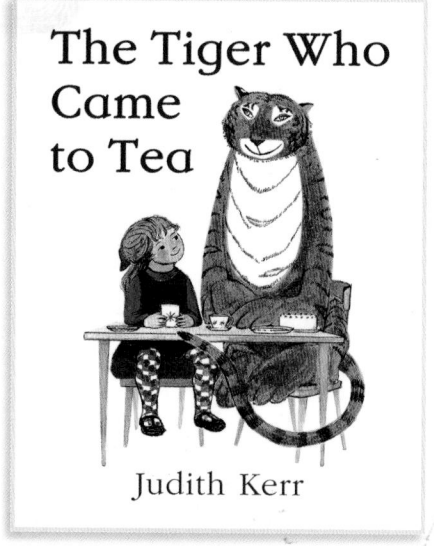

The Tiger Who Came to Tea

Judith Kerr

"A modern classic"
Independent

MOG the Forgetful Cat

Judith Kerr

"A national treasure"
Junior Magazine

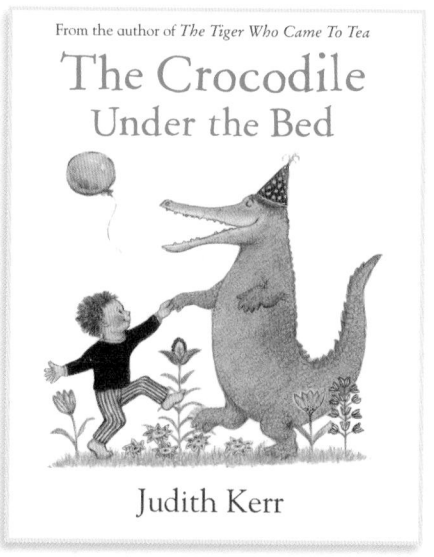

From the author of *The Tiger Who Came To Tea*

The Crocodile Under the Bed

Judith Kerr

"…full of the beauty, poetry and whimsy that has graced every piece of work she has created…" *Independent*

Also look out for

Mog in the Dark • Mog and the V. E.T. • Mog and the Granny • Mog's Christmas
Goodbye Mog • When Willy Went to the Wedding • The Other Goose • Goose in a Hole
Twinkles, Arthur and Puss • One Night in the Zoo • My Henry • The Great Granny Gang

Board Books also available:

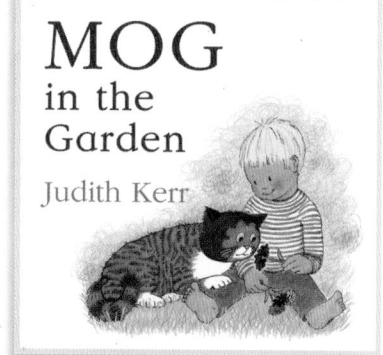

MOG in the Garden

Judith Kerr

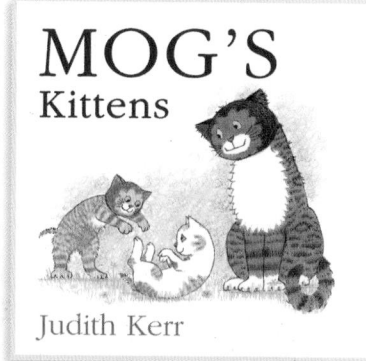

MOG'S Kittens

Judith Kerr

MOG'S Family of Cats

Judith Kerr

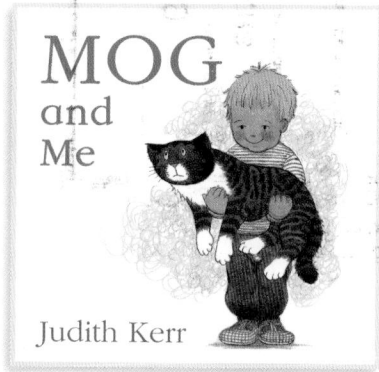

MOG and Me

Judith Kerr